You do not die.

Your soul steps out of your body, shakes itself hard because it's been carrying the weight of your heavy skin for fifteen years. Then your soul lifts up and looks down on your body lying there—looks down on the blood running onto concrete, your eyes snapped open like the pages in some kid's forgotten picture book, your chest not moving. Your soul sees this and feels something beyond sadness—feels its whole self whispering further away. It lifts you up—over a world of sadness and anger and fear. Over a world of first kisses and hands touching and someone you're falling in love with. She's there now. Right there. Look closely. Yeah. That's her. That's my Ellie....

OTHER BOOKS BY JACQUELINE WOODSON

The Dear One

The House You Pass on the Way

Hush

If You Come Softly

I Hadn't Meant to Tell You This

Lena

Locomotion

Miracle's Boys

Behind you

JACQUELINE WOODSON

speak

An Imprint of Penguin Group (USA) Inc.

SPEAK

Published by the Penguin Group

Penguin Group (USA) Inc., 345 Hudson Street, New York, New York 10014, U.S.A.

Penguin Group (Canada), 90 Eglinton Avenue East, Suite 700,
Toronto, Ontario, Canada M4P 2Y3 (a division of Pearson Penguin Canada Inc.)

Penguin Books Ltd, 80 Strand, London WC2R 0RL, England

Penguin Ireland, 25 St Stephen's Green, Dublin 2, Ireland
(a division of Penguin Books Ltd)

Penguin Group (Australia), 250 Camberwell Road, Camberwell, Victoria 3124, Australia
(a division of Pearson Australia Group Pty Ltd)

Penguin Books India Pvt Ltd, 11 Community Centre, Panchsheel Park,
New Delhi - 110 017, India

Penguin Group (NZ), Cnr Airborne and Rosedale Roads, Albany, Auckland 1310,
New Zealand (a division of Pearson New Zealand Ltd)

Penguin Books (South Africa) (Pty) Ltd, 24 Sturdee Avenue,
Rosebank, Johannesburg 2196, South Africa

Registered Offices: Penguin Books Ltd, 80 Strand, London WC2R 0RL, England

First published in the United States of America by G. P. Putnam's Sons,
a division of Penguin Young Readers Group, 2004
Published by Speak, an imprint of Penguin Group (USA) Inc., 2006

1 3 5 7 9 10 8 6 4 2

Poem on page vii from *All of Us: The Collected Poems* by Raymond Carver,
copyright © 1996 by Tess Gallagher. Introduction copyright © 1996 by Tess
Gallagher. Editor's preface, commentary, and notes copyright © 1996 by William L.
Stull. Used by permission of Alfred A. Knopf, a division of Random House, Inc.

THE LIBRARY OF CONGRESS HAS CATALOGED THE G. P. PUTNAM'S SONS EDITION AS FOLLOWS:

Woodson, Jacqueline.

Behind you / Jacqueline Woodson.

p. cm.

Summary: After fifteen-year-old Jeremiah is mistakenly shot by police, the people
who love him struggle to cope with their loss as they recall his life and death,
unaware that Miah is watching over them.

ISBN: 0-399-23988-X (hc)

[1. Death—Fiction. 2. Grief—Fiction. 3. Interpersonal relations—Fiction.
4. African Americans—Fiction. 5. New York (N.Y.)—Fiction.] I. Title.
PZ7.W84945Be 2004 [Fic]—dc22 2003023179

Speak ISBN 0-14-240390-3

Printed in the United States of America

For my family

And did you get what
you wanted from this life, even so?

I did.

And what did you want?

To call myself beloved, to feel myself
beloved on the earth.

—Raymond Carver

The Ending

Jeremiah

YOU DO NOT DIE. YOUR SOUL STEPS OUT OF YOUR BODY, shakes itself hard because it's been carrying the weight of your heavy skin for fifteen years. Then your soul lifts up and looks down on your body lying there—looks down on the blood running onto concrete, your eyes snapped open like the pages in some kid's forgotten picture book, your chest not moving. Your soul sees this and feels something beyond sadness—feels its whole self whispering further away. *Shhhh. Shhhh. Shhhh*—past the trees in Central Park, past the statues and runners and children playing on swings. *Shhhh. Shhhh. Shhhh.* Over yellow taxicabs and late-afternoon flickering streetlights. *Shhhh* away from the dusting of snow, the white tips of trees, the darkening sky. Already you hear your mother screaming. Already you see your father dropping his head into his hands.

3

Helpless. Already you see your friends—walking through the halls of Percy Academy. Stunned. But you do not die. Each breath your soul takes is cool and reminds you of a taste you loved a long time ago. Licorice. Peppermint. Rain. Then your soul is you all over again, only lighter and freer and able to be a thousand and one places at once. Your new soul eyes look around. See two cops standing there with their mouths hanging open. One cop curses and kicks a tree. Slowly your soul realizes it's in a park. There are trees all around you. And both cops look scared.

He's dead, one cop says.

And the other curses again. Your soul doesn't like the way the curse word sounds. Too hard. Too heavy in the new soul-light air.

The cops can't see you. They see a dead body on the ground—a young boy. A black boy. They know this is not the *man* they'd been looking for. They know they've made a mistake. Your soul looks at the boy and knows his friends called him Miah but his full name was Jeremiah Roselind. Tall. Dark. He has locks and the locks are spread over the ground. His eyes are opened wide. Greenish gray lifeless eyes. Your soul thinks—somebody loved that boy once. Thinks—once that boy was me. The wind blows the snow left, right and up. You are so light, you move with the wind and the snow. Let the weather take you. And it lifts you up—over a world of sadness and anger and fear. Over a world of first kisses and hands touching and someone you're falling in love with. She's there now. Right there. Look closely. Yeah. That's her. That's my Ellie.

The Hurting

Ellie

FOR A LONG TIME AFTER MIAH DIED, SO MANY PEOPLE DIDN'T sleep. At night, we lay in bed with our eyes wide open and watched the way night settled down over wherever we were. I was in a room on the Upper West Side, in a house my parents moved to a long time ago. Not a *house*—a duplex *apartment* in a fancy building with a doorman. My dad's a doctor. My mother stays at home. I go to Percy Academy. Some people look at me and see a white girl in a uniform—burgundy jacket and gray skirt—and think, *She has all the privilege in the world.* I look back at them, thinking, *If only you knew.*

If only they knew how we were sprinkled all over the city—me in my big room, Nelia in her Fort Greene brownstone, Norman in his girlfriend's apartment, aunts and uncles and cousins, even strangers—all over New York City—none of us slept. We lay there staring up at our ceilings or out into the darkness. Or some days we stopped in the middle of doing something and forgot what it was we were doing. We thought, *Jeremiah's dead.* We whispered, *Jeremiah's dead.* As if the whispering and the thinking could help us to understand. We didn't eat enough. We peed only when the need to pee got so big, we thought we'd wet our pants. We pulled the covers off ourselves in the mornings then sat on the edge of our beds, not knowing what to do next. If those strangers looked, really looked into my privileged white girl face, they would have seen the place where I wasn't even there. Where a part of me died too.

Miah died on a Saturday afternoon. That evening, the calls started coming. First his mom, Nelia, asking if Miah was still with me. Then his dad, Norman. Then the cops. Then silence. Silence that lasted into the night and into the next dawn. Then the phone ringing one more time and Nelia saying, *Ellie, Miah's been shot. . . .*

I don't remember much more than that. There was a funeral. There were tears. There were days and days spent in my bed. A fever maybe.

There was no more Miah.

No more Miah.

No more Miah and me.

Nelia

I USED TO BE A WRITER. IDEAS AND PEOPLE AND PLACES WOULD come to me and I'd write it all down. There was such a *clarity* to the world then. When I sat down at my desk and began to write, I felt like I understood *everything*. I felt brilliant and whole and good. But who understands *everything*. Who understands *anything*. I mean *really*. People getting awards for being geniuses and brilliant writers and world shakers. Do they understand. Do they have any *idea* what it feels like to wake up some days not even sure of your own name. What is my name? . . . Nelia. It's Nelia. My whole name? Cornelia Elizabeth Roselind. But before it was Roselind, it was something else. This morning, I don't remember. It doesn't matter anyway. Who I was. Who I am. Who I'll be one day. You see, the whole world has changed for me. It's filled with people saying things I don't understand. Faces on the television screen talk at me—lips moving with no sound. There's a war somewhere. And somewhere else, there are suicide bombers. People missing and found. Children looking for homes. Candy for sale. This morning, I saw a dog with only three legs. It was black and had the saddest eyes. But what dog isn't sad eyed. And what child doesn't want a home. My skin used to be so soft. But now I feel like a hard shell is growing over my blood and bones. *The New York Times* grows like a sunflower just inside the vestibule. It gets delivered in a blue plastic bag. A blue sunflower, growing out of control. But I can't stop it from growing. Someone needs to come to this house. Teach me how to dial a phone again. Because then I could call someone—who?—and say—what? Please don't deliver any more papers. Is that what you say? When a person answers the phone—do you ask for *less* of something? Who wants *less* of something? Don't we all want more?

I am not old. My hair is still black. The way it curls has not changed. Except in one spot. There. Right where the tiny indent of my neck bends into my head. The hair is straight there. Once it used to curl and the curls moved toward my neck. But now the hair sticks straight down like someone's bad perm job.

And my hands. I am not old, but my hands shake

sometimes. I cannot find a pen that writes. I cannot find paper to write on. I cannot. I cannot. I cannot.

So I sleep. In this big house with all of its quiet, what else is there to do?

Kennedy

LOST OUR LAST GAME UP AGAINST DALTON LAST WINTER, 102–62. Dalton don't have no game. I mean, that team is *busted*. People trying to say it's 'cause Miah got kilt—killed—I mean, he got *killed*. But even if Miah's dead, that ain't no reason to get your booty *slammed* by some I-don't-want-no-scrubs from *Dalton*. I mean, show a dead brother some respect and at least go into some overtime or somethin'. Don't be just straight-up losing like that.

I'ma tell you—there's things I love about Percy Academy and stuff that be making me crazy. Like the team. I mean, I love ball, but Percy got the A-1 sorriest team this side of, I don't know—this side of the *galaxy*. Probably got a better team dribbling down the Milky Way. Three-inch Martians probably got better jump shots than the guys on my team. But there's stuff I love about that school too. Like—okay, so I know this is whacked and if someone said

I said it, I'd be ready to mess them up real bad and nobody'd believe them anyway 'cause everybody at Percy knows Kennedy don't be playing that, but . . . I love the uniforms. Carlos be saying, *There goes Kennedy in his monkey suit,* but I know it's just jealousy eating him up from the inside out. See, where I live, don't a whole lotta kids be going to private school. Kids be going to school— it ain't like how reporters be trying to televise—all that talk about high dropout rate and teenage pregnancy and blasé, blasé . . . Yeah, that goes on where I live, but it be going on where everybody else be living too. Only trouble is—the news got a need to be slanting stuff just to make people afraid. Like if peeps ain't running around scared enough as it is. I just hate that the news gotta be making people afraid of somebody that look like me. Or Miah. If Miah's really dead, then that's the reason—he's dead because of people being afraid. That's why I don't try to be afraid of nothing. In the morning I get up, brush my teeth, take a shower. I look in the mirror and take off my nylon, check my braids, make sure they working underneath it. Maybe if my scalp's dry, I'll run a little bit of grease in the parts, spray a little oil sheen on my braids— you know, make them nice. Then I put on my Percy clothes: gray pants—I wear them baggy, the school don't trip, so that's cool—white shirt with a maroon tie. Maroon jacket got a Percy Academy patch on the left breast. Walk out of building 1633 Albany Houses in NeverRan Never-Will Brownsville. Brooklyn, New York. Yeah—it's the projects. Yeah, I come from the projects. So what? Lots of Percy kids got heavy pockets, live in those big buildings on the Upper East Side and the Upper West Side. They be having doormen and dry cleaning dropped off and what-not. Stuff like that. I guess some of them probably think they better than me because they got some cash and what-ever, whatever. But truth is, cash and doormen and some nice clothes ain't gonna be going with you to the next place. Shoot—given the fact that we gotta wear uniforms at Percy, nice clothes don't even be getting you through *this* place. Yeah, I believe in a next place. And I believe in this place too. And when I'm sitting in my room, staring up at the posters of all the ballplayers that came before me—I start understanding that I know some things. I might not be real rich or real smart or real good looking, but I know some things. I know a cop shot Miah in the back and the bullet went straight through from his shoul-der blade to his heart. And then the heart just turned it-self off like a TV. And maybe it burned Miah to die that way. Maybe it hurt real bad going down like that. But some days, I feel my boy right here, right next to me. He's sitting on my bed. And he's looking up at the posters too. And he's got this big grin on his face. I even feel his

16

hand—slapping mine, saying, *You know we shoulda whipped Dalton, yo.* And I take his hand, pull him to me real quick, slap his back. Say, *Who you tellin', Miah man? Who you tellin'?*

Norman Roselind

THE SNOW STARTED MELTING IN JANUARY. AFTER THAT CAME the rain. Jeremiah'd been dead about a month and a half by then. Each day, I looked out the window expecting to see some sun, but it didn't come for a long time. Shoot. It was like Miah died and the sun just changed its mind about shining. City so gray, it could've been Seattle. Pain in me so deep, some days I just stood wherever I was, my mouth hanging open, my eyes burning up. My heart always just banging and banging. All these years I hadn't thought about it, and then my son died and my heart started pounding, always, like it wanted to break right through my chest. Even as I'm telling this, it's banging. Doctors say nothing they can do about this feeling. And I know they're looking at me, wanting to say—*We can't bring him back, Mr. Roselind.*

So the world just stayed gray, my eyes burn, and then some days the tears come and don't stop, and then some days it's just my heart, banging and banging like that.

But I'm talking about that winter, right after everything. I was trying to do the things a person does to keep moving—dry cleaners, auto repair, post office . . . I'd taken a roll of film to get developed and when I got it back, there were some pictures in there from that day me and Miah had gone for a drive out to East Hampton because I was looking at this location to shoot my next movie. I don't want anybody to ever have to imagine what it's like to walk out of a drugstore with an envelope full of pictures under their arm—then, when they open that envelope, all they see is picture after picture of their dead son. I wouldn't wish that on anybody—no matter how deep my dislike of that person went. But that was me, walking up Fulton Street, my throat closing up so tight, I had to stop walking, remember how to breathe again. I remember a little girl and her mother crossed the street when they saw me standing there like that. Another woman asked if I was all right. I said, *My son . . . my son was killed. Jeremiah. My son was Jeremiah. He was only fifteen. Only fifteen.* I kept saying that. *Only fifteen.* And the tears came and wouldn't stop. The woman wanted to know what my address was and somehow I was able to tell her. She put her hand under my elbow and slowly led me home. Lois Ann was there. She thanked the woman. Took me upstairs and got me into bed. That was a long time ago. Some days it feels like it just happened.

In one of the pictures, Miah's got this big grin on his face. When I started going through those pictures, it took me right back to that day. Made me remember that we'd been having this whole talk about white people and I'd said something about white people not knowing they were white. Like if they go to a party, they don't know they're white if it's all white people in the room, but if they go to a party of black folks—*then* they know. I remember Miah getting quiet and staring out the window. He was wearing a green jacket and his black jeans. I remember looking over at him and thinking, *How did me and Nelia make such a beautiful child?* But he wasn't a child anymore. There was just the thinnest road of hair going across his top lip and his face had changed—he had my jawline— sharp. And he had the same habit I have of clenching his teeth when he was thinking real hard on something. We drove for a bit, him staring and clenching, me wondering what was on his mind.

"You don't think there's one white person in this world, Daddy," Miah said, "somewhere, who's different? Who gets up in the morning and says, 'I'm white, so what am I gonna do with this—how am I going to use it to change the world?' "

Now I know why he was asking. Know why we were having that talk that day. But what good is it that I know now?

Jeremiah

THE SOUL LOOKS BACK AND WONDERS. MINE DID. ONLY I didn't know it was my soul—I thought it was me looking back at me. But I kept hearing my grandmother's voice. The way she'd say that—*The soul looks back and wonders*—every time something made no sense to her. Or every time I did something that seemed completely outrageous. Like the time I put a plastic snake on top of her laundry pile. She got so scared, she couldn't even catch her breath. And her sitting there with her hand on her chest breathing hard in and out made me realize—even at seven years old—that I'd done something there wasn't any turning back from. That the way she was gonna beat my butt once she finally *did* catch her breath was gonna be like no butt whipping I'd ever felt before. Or would ever feel again, thank goodness. And later on, as she took the strap to my bare legs and sore behind, she kept saying,

"The soul"—*slap*—"looks"—*slap*—"back"—*slap*—
"and"—*slap*—"wonders"—*slap*.

My grandmother could beat a behind, yo. That's no joke. She'd get this look on her face when you got fresh, or got caught playing with matches, or put a snake on her laundry. And the look was like "Where in God's name did you ever get an idea that that was the right thing to . . . " And then you knew. You knew it was all over for your behind. My mom and pops never laid a hand on me, but my grandma made up for their non-whipping parenting by letting me know every now and then that

"In order to be raised right, Jeremiah—you can*not* spare the rod."

I was her only grandchild and she loved me with this love so fierce, my pops used to say you could feel it coming on for miles. Soon as we got a call saying she was on her way up to New York, my pops would say,

"Stand still, Miah. You feel the love coming?"

Desire Viola Roselind

FOR EIGHT YEARS I WAS MIAH'S GRAM. BEFORE THAT TOO, I reckon. Feels like I've known him since before he got to the world—longer than he knew himself, truthfully. Seems like we'd been friends really—not gram and first-born grandson—somewhere before life on earth . . .

Life. On. Earth.

Think on that. Earth looks small from far'ways. I remember when I was a child and my daddy showed me a blue marble, those kind that don't just have blue in them but lots of other colors besides. He says to me, *Girl, look hard at this here marble, 'cause what you looking at is the whole wide world.*

And I looked hard at the marble and then I looked real hard at my pa and I reckon I must have been thinking that here's a man I always loved who's lost his mind.

We lived in Aiken then. A little brick house. You went

up three stone stairs and then you were on our porch. And there was a swing on the porch—old iron swing that squealed to high heaven every time you sat down on it and commenced to swinging. Well, you went up those three stone stairs and passed that porch swing and then you were at our front screen door. Then you were in our front room—hardwood floors, a big potbellied stove— stove warmed the house like you wouldn't believe. One year, my baby sister set fire to her own dress sleeve standing too close to the open stove door. The skin on her arm was never the same after that, and she carried that arm sort of different from the other. When she got to be a young woman, she never wore short sleeves—not even in the hottest months—because she was ashamed. Don't know if the shame come from the scars or from her childhood foolishness of sticking her arm in the fire. Reckon it had to be some of both. Guess that's my first recollection of how people hide their scars.

Girl, my daddy said, *I know you think I lost my mind, but this marble is how the world looks to everybody but us humans.*

I looked at the marble. I looked at my daddy. I looked around at our little brick house. Back and forth and back and forth like that till I must have looked some kind of foolish myself.

Sir, I said, *I reckon I don't know what you mean when*

you say everybody but us humans. Ain't nobody else but God to see.

Uh-uh, Sweet Pea, my daddy said. He'd been squatting down, sitting back on his haunches like a lot of people used to do. He'd sit that way, squatted down, 'cause he was tall—over six feet—and me and my sisters and brothers had gotten our mama's gift for not growing tall. I was the smallest in the family—tiny hands, tiny feet and body.

Well, my daddy stood up and looked down on me and let himself smile. He had a nice, big, white-toothed smile, my daddy did.

Close your eyes, my daddy said.

I did.

And just let yourself think, Sweet Pea. Think about this world without its color and sound and smells. Let your breathing stop a moment.

I did.

Now commence to breathing again and open up those eyes.

I did.

And here is the whole wide world again. But better now, isn't it?

I looked around, and I liked the way it felt to have everything back in its place, the way the room came back in view and the floor felt hard again. And my daddy standing there grinning like he would be that way . . . always. . . .

And now, here I am—way on the other side of that story and that beautiful day. I grew up and I grew old and then I got sickly and I died. But before all that happened, I had me a son, and that son had himself a son. And he named that boy-child Jeremiah.

And some mornings, Jeremiah comes to where I'm sitting, rocking in this big maple chair, the cushion softer than any cushion should ever be, the wood smelling like it was cut only an hour ago, the air cool and gentle as a child's hand. And Miah sits down beside me and we look out before us where the rest of the world is hustling past—people doing what they need to be doing to get through their days.

And Jeremiah says, *Tell me that story again, Grandma, the one about the marble.*

And the love in my heart for that boy-child just fills up inside me and spills all over.

Ellie

THE FIRST TIME I TRIED TO WALK TO THE PLACE WHERE THE cops shot Miah, it was dark. Central Park is not a safe place at night. People have been mugged. Raped. One man was attacked by a group of kids who just wanted to see if they could get away with it—rich kids from the Upper East Side. Some of them got away, but three were caught. *We were just playing,* they said. *We didn't think it would end that way.* Well, that man didn't make it. I don't know what happened to the kids—kids my age—fifteen, sixteen. The news was all over the story for a while and then it wasn't anymore. Something else must've happened and the media's absolute glee followed that new thing. The park at night is dark and quiet, though. If it wasn't for the danger, it would be a beautiful place. I wanted to see where Miah fell. I wanted to listen—hear him crying out. Two months had passed since his dying. It was late February and so cold, my hands hurt. I knew the place—the papers had reported the story for almost a month. There had been demonstrations—yet another black guy shot in a case of mistaken identity. But this had been different. According to the papers, Miah was not just some black guy. He was a rich kid. He was the kid of famous parents. He was loved and attended one of the most prestigious schools in New York City. I read every word, even when Marion tried to take the papers from me.

"You don't need to do this to yourself, Elisha," she said.

"Yes, I do," I said back. Yes, she is my mother. But she doesn't understand. How could she ever understand any of it? How could anyone know what it was like? It was all so damned useless. And the stupid papers—how dare they? How dare they measure one life against another.

The first time I tried to walk to the place where the cops shot Miah, a dog ran out from nowhere, then darted back into the darkness. I stopped, a long way away from that place—in the dark and in the cold. I stopped, hugged myself hard in the darkness.

And screamed and screamed and screamed.

Carlton

THAT SATURDAY AFTERNOON—I'LL ALWAYS CALL IT THAT. That Saturday. Not "The Day Miah Died." Not "The Day a Whole Lot of Us Changed Forever." Not "Saturday, December Eighth." That Saturday, the snow started coming down hard. I had been sitting on the stoop just thinking on things. That fall, I'd begun to realize this thing about me, this stupid secret thing that I knew I'd never live out or talk about. And then the fall was over and it was starting to snow. A new season. Different weather and the secret getting older and deeper. When the snow started falling, it was wetter and colder than I'd ever remembered it being. I had on a sweater and some jeans and my hiking boots. Maybe I had on a T-shirt underneath, but it wasn't enough. Even my fingernails were cold. I looked over at Jeremiah's building—every window except Nelia's study was dark. I knew Miah wasn't home, so I couldn't go over there. But I didn't want to go inside my own house. My mother was inside and she was probably reading on the couch. A romance novel. She was probably reading about a woman who fell in love with a man and lived happily ever after. The books with the shiny gold letters on them. Always white women. My mother's white and I wonder if she sees some part of herself in those books—wonder if she makes wishes. Or just lets herself get caught up in them before coming back to planet Earth to make dinner for me and my dad and start ironing her clothes for the next week of working. She teaches. My father plays music. They've been together forever. My sister's in England. Oxford. She wanted to get out of New York. Wanted to get away from our tiny family, I guess. Maybe I was thinking about all of this as I sat there shivering and singing real low. Maybe it's because my dad's a musician that I like to sing. There's always been music in my house. That day, I was singing "Landslide"—not the remake, but the old Fleetwood Mac version where Stevie Nicks really rocks it. Jeremiah always thought it was strange that I was such a Stevie Nicks fan, but her voice— her *voice*—it did something to you. And no one can do "Landslide" the way she does. My father had turned me on to that song. He plays piano and guitar and a couple of other instruments. He'd sit down with his guitar and just start strumming and singing that song. *Can I sail through the changing ocean tide? Can I handle the seasons of my life?* And there was always such a sadness in his voice, but nothing compared to Stevie's. When she starts going on about the landslide bringing her down, it snaps the heart. So I sat there, singing, trying to do what she did with that song.

But then something strange happened. I forgot the words. I had been hearing and singing that song my whole life, and there I was, sitting in the heavy, wet snow, not knowing the lyrics to a song that was like the *alphabet* to me. And I looked around, starting to feel a panic build up. The block was empty and getting dark. The snow was coming down hard. And then I remember thinking, *And where the hell is Miah?*

The Healing

Norman Roselind

Sᴜɴᴅᴀʏ ᴍᴏʀɴɪɴɢ, I ʜᴇᴀʀ ᴛʜᴇ sᴏᴜɴᴅ ᴏꜰ ᴛʜᴇ *Tɪᴍᴇs* ʜɪᴛᴛɪɴɢ the stoop. It's still early and looks like it's going to rain. My girlfriend's still asleep. I look over at her as I'm rising out of bed. Her hair's getting gray and her cheeks are starting to puff a little bit with age. Wonder what she sees when she looks at me. I look at my hands, the way they still shake most days, the way my whole body trembles sometimes until I think relaxing thoughts—oceans and forests and cool, lazy evenings. Still, my heart bangs against my chest. And my eyes, I know when a person looks into them, they see only half a man—not completely focused, not completely there. I touch my girlfriend's back, watch my trembling hand move down over it. She's a beautiful woman—brown skinned, dark eyed, enough meat on her bones not to ever be called skinny. Has a voice like something cool calling your name. The trembling slows, then stops, and I rise, pull my robe on over my pajamas and go downstairs to get the paper.

When I open the door, I look up at Nelia's window. I used to be married to her. And we used to have a son. I feel my hands start to tremble again and think, *That's the past now. Move on.* There's a dull ache in my head. I pull the plastic off the paper and look at the headlines without reading them. So much news. So many things to do in a day. So many people to remember. And birthdays and holidays coming up. Eggs and milk to buy. Miah wore a size eleven shoe. My hands. My head. Lake Erie. Lake Champlain. The way the water laps against the shore on Montauk. Miah's brown hands building a sand castle. His thin seven-year-old body. *Daddy, look!* And the wave coming up that afternoon. The way he laughed as the castle melted into the ocean. Where was that? St. Croix? Mauritius?

Nelia's curtains are pulled—they've been that way for some time now. The papers were piling up on her stoop, but now they're all gone. She lives just across the street and a few houses up. It wasn't supposed to end like this. I wasn't supposed to fall in love with Lois Ann. Some things just happen and you feel them happening but you don't have a whole lot of power over them happening. You have to kind of give yourself over to them. Maybe me and Nelia were moving apart for a long time. It's hard to look back on. The edges of the past get fuzzy when I try. Moments come clear—the first time I heard my newborn son cry. The way his eyes changed to the same color as Nelia's and him with parts of Nelia and parts of me all running together to make some strange and wonderful whole new being. He really was *something*.

I sit down on the stoop and try to read the *Times*. The president wants a war. Some businessmen have been stealing people's retirement funds. A baby found, left beside a grade school. The baby's fine. The schoolkids all want her to be named after them. I read this story and even with all of its ugliness, I can't help smiling. Kids are something. All they can see is the beauty in a moment. I sit there like that awhile—every once in a while looking up at Nelia's window. Feel like I've been making films all my life and none of them can tell the whole story. I'd love to make one—just one—movie that goes from the beginning to the end—tell-all. And not that greasy talk-show tell-all kind of thing, but you know, go to the heart—to the heart's heart—and let the world feel everything deep like that.

Now the curtain in Nelia's living room moves a bit. I want to say, *Open the window, Nelia. Open the doors. Come outside. It's autumn.* This morning is cool and beautiful. The trees are starting to change color. *Look, honey,* I want to say. *Look how the world is moving on.*

Nelia

IT RAINED THE FIRST MORNING ELLIE RANG MY BELL. IN THE city, the rain makes the world gray and then the sun shines down on that gray and everything echoes of silver. Such a beautiful metal, silver is. And downstairs, Ellie stood draped in it, her thick black hair damp, her clothes wet, her long, thin body shivering.

It's Ellie, she said, looking up at the window. Looking up at me.

Then Ellie smiled. Her beautiful Ellie smile and a moment, a moment from a long time ago draped itself over me: my Jeremiah and Ellie in that spot where Ellie was standing. Ellie turning toward Jeremiah and offering my son that smile. I felt old watching them through the window. Old but excited—like I was fifteen again too and turning toward some boy—who would it have been?— and smiling.

"Ellie," I said. "Ellie, it's good to see you." My voice sounded so foreign to me. An old lady's voice. When had I become old? A birthday had passed, but still . . .

How long had it been since Jeremiah's last day with us—a month, two months, a year. Maybe Ellie knew. Maybe Ellie would tell me.

But once inside, she put her hands in the pockets of her jeans and looked around. The smile gone now. What was she seeing? The gray, dusty inside of what was once a beautiful home. The darkness. One by one, the lightbulbs had burned out. Now I flicked switches and got nothing.

"It's kinda dark in here," Ellie said. And then the smile was back. There was something different to it, though—embarrassment around the mouth and at the edges of the eyes. "How about we light some candles."

She followed me into the kitchen, where I pulled dusty white votive candles from a drawer.

"The matches are over the stove."

Ellie walked over to the stove. To the left of her was the window that looked out over our block. Yellow stained-glass panes across the top of it. A yellow linen curtain hanging from it. Dusty. Still. Ellie pulled it back, the matches in her other hand forgotten.

"He loved the light in this room," she said, her voice almost a whisper. I watched her thin hand reach up to the yellow panes, her pale skin soften in their light. In the cloudy rain-light coming in from the window, I could see that her fingers were long and the nails were painted a soft pink. I wondered when she had done this. Late at night? In the morning? Was she thinking of Jeremiah as she brushed the color on? Whom did she make herself beautiful for these days?

She kept her hand on the glass, oblivious of me. The kitchen grew terribly silent, a silence I had come to know too well. And now, with Ellie in it with me, the silence didn't seem to belong. But I stood there in it. Watching Ellie's hand touch the glass. I stood there, wearing the same khaki pants I had been wearing for I don't know how many days, the same white T-shirt I don't remember ever pulling over my head. The day after Miah's funeral, I marched to the Fulton Street Barbershop and had them cut off all of my hair. Who needed hair? Who needed anything? But now, I let my hand reach up to my head and felt that the hair had grown in some, long enough now for me to grab a handful of it. As I did this, something strange happened—the sun, which had been watery and elusive all morning, turned sharp and bright, spreading a thin layer of brilliant yellow over everything. I kept my hand in my hair and slowly looked around the kitchen—at the yellow dust covering everything, the cedar chairs draped in yellow light, the battered, beautiful wooden table with yellow swimming across it, the white walls looking as though they'd been dipped in butter . . .

Ellie turned then, and for a moment we just stared at each other. The air had left me. I felt ragged suddenly—hollow. I wanted to scream into the yellow light. Yet—it held me . . . up and together.

"He . . . ," Ellie said again, looking directly at me. "He really did love this light."

Carlton

September. The leaves are starting to come down. The sky—the sky seems like it's just *this* much closer to the earth. It's cool today but still warm enough for me not to wear a jacket. This—this is the kind of day a guy can fall in love with. If I could marry a day, it would be a day in September—the kind of day that makes you feel kind of blue and kind of crazy all at once. But you can't marry a day. My mother married a night. My father. Carlton Sr. Black man. And me, born a color somewhere between my blue-eyed white mother and dark-skinned dad. What if the color white was a day? And what if my mother had married a day instead of a night? Then I'd be all white. I wouldn't be walking through this September day, choking up at falling leaves. Would I be alone?

Someone dies and you hold on to everything you can. I think it's easier if you know they're gonna die—somebody old who you loved—like a grandmother or a sweet old uncle. You watch them die, you expect their death, and while death is coming, you're getting stories from them and touching their skin one last time and smiling and telling them how much you love them. But when someone gets killed—the way my homeboy Miah got killed—shot down by cops in a case of mistaken identity—sounds clichéd even to say it. Wish it was a cliché. Wish it was a dream that I could wake up from, shake out of my head and say, *Now where did that come from.* No. No dream. When someone gets killed, when that someone is this guy you've spent just about every day with since you were this high—well, then you don't see it coming. And all you have to hold on to is what you remember— and the day. The light of it. The weather. You in it. The way everything about it smells and feels and looks. Then you go to bed at night feeling like you lived it, really lived it. Like you walked through the world that day—whole. When somebody dies real quick and unexpectedly like Miah did, you spend every single day, after the news hits you, trying to live. And maybe sometimes you're living with some big secrets over your head or some big regrets in your heart. But the good part is you're walking and breathing and waving hello. And as the days go by and turn into weeks and months and years, you realize how much each day you get through matters.

I take a deep breath and keep walking. Still day. Wind-less day. Day with so much color to it, my head starts to ache. But then the color softens. It feels as though the whole sky is trying to wrap itself around me. I stop, lean against a mailbox and take small breaths. And it feels like the air is trying to breathe with me. *Calm Carlton,* the air feels like it's saying. *Why you gotta be so high-strung anyway.* But it's not the air—it's Miah. I hear his voice, feel him grinning. Then I'm grinning too. Headache gone quickly as it came. *Why you gotta be so high-strung.*

"Miss you, man," I whisper.

A little boy passing by me stops.

"You talking to me?"

He's brown like Miah. Clean-cut. Neater than any lit-tle boy should be.

I shake my head and he shrugs and keeps on moving. *You ain't all gone, are you, Miah?*

And the wind starts blowing, soft and high as a song.

At the corner of South Oxford and Fulton, a car swerves to miss hitting a small dog. I hear the dog's owner scream and watch her curse the driver out. Then he's curs-ing back and the cars behind him are honking and the day doesn't seem as beautiful as it did a minute ago.

I keep walking. When I get to Vanderbilt and Fulton, I stop and think about grabbing a cup of coffee. At a red light, some scrub leans out of the passenger side of a beatdown Honda and says *Hey, Girl-boy*. He winks at me. I hear the other guys in the car laugh.

"You weren't calling me that last night," I say. And wink back at him. The guys in the back start howling and the scrub gets so mad, he makes a move to get out of the car, but the light changes and his friend speeds off.

I keep walking. Girl-boy. Fag. Batty-boy. The list goes on. I've heard it all before. I remember me and Miah were walking this one time and some guy he knew from somewhere pulled him to the side and whispered, loud enough for me to hear, "What you hanging with the sissies for, Miah-man?"

Miah had his ball in his hand—the way he usually did. He chucked it to me and grinned.

"Take some inventory, man," Miah said to the guy. "Everything in the world's just a little bit deeper than you seeing it."

The guy walked off without saying anything else. I know he didn't have a clue to what Miah was talking about, but maybe he walked on thinking about it some. I don't know.

Did me and Miah ever talk about this? About *it*. About who I really am—you know, way down deep beneath the me that's part white, part black, a ballplayer, a singer, a pretty-boy?

Nah. We didn't. We left that stuff alone. We talked

about ball and our folks and more ball. And when Miah started falling in love with Ellie, we talked about that—about what it meant to be a black guy who was loving a white girl. And once we got on that subject, it was like—well, it was like that's all there was, because he and I could spend hours just talking about people's reactions and his own fears and what it felt like to just be with Ellie. He loved that girl. I'd sit talking with him and then I'd come home to my parents sitting on the couch, watching TV—sometimes my dad would have his arm around my mom's shoulders. And I'd think, *Man, I can't even hardly imagine it, but these two old people were, like, our age one time and they got some of those same funky stares and comments Miah and Ellie got.*

So with all that going on, where was there a place to say, *You know, Miah, I don't think I'm the kind of guy that likes girls.*

But now that Miah's gone, I find myself having all kinds of conversations with him. Telling him when I first started feeling this way, how lonely I've been all these years, how all the stuff I don't say and don't do goes into ballplaying and that's probably why I'm on the starting five and one of the best ballplayers in the history of Brooklyn Technical High School. Stupid name for a school that's supposed to be one of the best in all of New York

City. Decent ball team, though, and some smart kids running through it.

I miss Miah so much, it hurts—real deep some days and other days it's just a hollowness. *You'll get close to someone again like that,* my mom said. It was one of those rare moments when we sat down at the table together—her drinking coffee, me eating a piece of leftover pie. But even though I sat at the kitchen table and nodded as she talked, on and on, trying to make me feel less of the sadness, I knew she was wrong—would always be wrong about that.

You won't always be the beautiful lonely boy you are, Carlton.

Beautiful-lonely—that's what my mother calls me. She knows even though we never spoke about it. She watches me watching people. Watches me walk and sing and talk. Comes to my games and watches me watching other ballplayers. She knows. Looks at me sideways and smiles a little bit when my father says, "When you gonna bring a girl up in this house for us to look at?"

"That's Carlton's business, isn't it?" my mother says. Because she knows. And she doesn't want my father to know before I'm ready to tell. Before I'm a hundred percent sure myself. About this. About that. About everything.

I wish I could love a girl the way Miah loved Ellie, **but** I just don't think about them that way—girls. I just don't. I try to force myself to—try to imagine my lips on a girl's, my arms around her waist, my hands making designs on her back. But the thoughts drip down into nothing. I feel . . . nothing. I am . . . nothing.

Jeremiah

IN A CLASSROOM IN A SCHOOL AROUND THE CORNER FROM where I grew up, a teacher is explaining death to seven-year-olds. Over the summer, the class hamster has died. A girl in the class has lost a beloved grandmother and another, an uncle. One kid remembers me and tells the class again how this guy he knows was shot by cops.

And he wasn't even doing nothing, the kid says. *Just running home from his girlfriend's house.*

Death, the teacher says. *Death is like sleep.*

Maybe there are twenty-five kids in the classroom—they're all colors because this neighborhood is changing fast. Even in the few months since I've died, it's changed. More white people moving in. Old black folks who've been here forever moving back down south or back to the Caribbean. The walls in this classroom are the same, though—painted pale blue. A poster on the wall—a kitten hanging from a bar—and underneath the kitten, the words HANG IN THERE. Another poster with the alphabet written in cursive. I remember being a kid and walking into this room, looking around wide-eyed, holding tight to my mama's hand. The room still smells like chalk. The chairs have names scratched into them. The desks are new, though, particle board and some kind of wood veneer that adds a new smell to the classroom, an unfamiliar one.

A little boy raises his hand. He could be me. Same dark skin. Same close haircut, shaped up on the sides and across his forehead. He's wearing a very white T-shirt and new-looking blue pants. His face is scrubbed and shining with oil. Today's the first day of school. Second grade. Twenty-something second-graders and all of them clean and excited and hungry for whatever is coming.

If death is like sleeping, the little boy says—his name is William, William Carlos—named, yes, for the poet. *If death is like sleeping, then how come dead people don't just wake up?*

I stare into his teacher's eyes. A flicker across them—she is stumped—but she recovers quickly.

It's a deeper sleep, she says.

Twenty-something pairs of eyes look back at her. Twenty-something children who won't sleep well tonight.

William Carlos looks at her. The others look at her, their mouths slightly open.

And then death comes, I want to say to them, *and you hang on.* And for a long time you don't even know you're dead and you're walking around in some strange place, staggering, asking everybody you meet—*Where am I? Where am I?* Then you see your long-dead grandma . . . and you know.

I want to let go—want to be whole on the other side of living. But life has a river running through it and we're all of us—dead and otherwise—on it together, linked up to one another. I want to stop looking. But I can't. I just can't. So I get up off that poor teacher's desk. Leave her sitting there with all those eyes on her.

When I was a kid, I learned this poem by Robert Frost and one of the lines in it was something about miles to go before I sleep. . . . Everybody seemed to have some different interpretation for that line. I don't remember the whole poem anymore, but I understand that line. If death is like sleeping, then I got a long way to go before I'm completely gone.

And that's what I'm thinking as I move out into the world. I turn and take one more look at William Carlos— his clear brown skin, his wide dark eyes. Future like a big empty trick-or-treat bag at the beginning of Halloween night.

Kennedy

IT TAKES ME AN HOUR AND FIFTEEN MINUTES TO GET HERE from Brownsville. Three trains, then a bit of a hike. But I've never been absent and I've never been late. My moms says, *Each day you go to that school is a gift, Kennedy.* She's never been up here. Says she don't have the right clothes. I didn't ask God to make me smart and a good ballplayer. He just did. And then lots of schools was saying, "Come here." "No, come here!" And then I was at Percy. But my heart's in Brownsville—with my moms and my boys and the Albany Houses. No matter where I go, I'm always gonna come back there. Ain't gonna be one of those kids that be leaving where they came from behind and making believe they came from a better place. I know people look at where I live and think all kinds of negative about it. They see people with a lot of kids and guys playing their music loud and smoking spliffs and that kind of stuff. They see us with our hair braided and our pants hanging low and they just think we all bad and whatever. My pops used to get mad when people would say I was "gifted." He'd say, "Nah—me and his mama the ones who got the gift—God sent us Kennedy." He used to think that was the funniest thing for some reason. And now some days I think about him saying that and I start grinning. The way my pops saw it, I was just like everybody else in these buildings—only thing is I got a real good game and somebody told me I was smart a long time ago and I believed it and started acting like it on paper—you know—doing my homework and stuff like that. Pulled down good grades. Teachers be surprised to see me with my hair braided, talking junk with my boys, then getting perfect marks on my spelling tests. My pops worked at a dry cleaner—pressing shirts and stuff. He didn't finish high school and he always wanted to go back or at least get a GED or something. It never happened, though. He used to say, "If somebody would go to each of the peeps up in these houses and say, 'You're something real special,' or something like that, no telling how many brothers and sisters would be jumping out of these doorways into college and probably even graduate school." I was a little kid then and didn't really believe him. But I do now. I don't know about being special or gifted or whatnot. I know *I'm lucky,* that's for sure. Ain't nothing special about luck—especially if you someone who doesn't have any.

Tuesday morning, I sat on the Percy stairs counting faces—white, white, white, white, white, Asian, Asian, white, black—Yo, what's up! (slap hands)—white, white, white, mixed kid—smiled at me, he's cool—white, white. . . . It went like that. When I got tired of counting faces, I took out some math homework and started looking it over, trying to wipe out the thoughts eating up my head. It was cool out—almost the end of September—one of those kinda days where you see a lot of people on blades and bicycles and walking around holding hands. The stairs go across the whole front of the school and even though the headmaster's always sending us notes about how we shouldn't be sitting on them because it makes the school look bad, everybody sits on them and nobody gets in trouble for it.

They hired this new math teacher that's crazy, but I think he's cool. He started writing all kinds of stuff on the board and I was like, *Yo, slow down and explain something, 'cause I'm lost as hot sauce.* Then the class laughed and he laughed, but he did slow down.

I sat there trying to figure out some math stuff when Ellie walked up and sat down next to me.

This okay, she said.

Free country, I said back. I don't really be talking to many peeps at Percy. I keep mostly to myself. Even though I play ball, I don't really be hanging with the ballplayers much either. When Miah was still living, me and him wasn't tight, but it wasn't nothing negative in it. He was different from me. I knew his dad was this famous film producer. And his moms was a writer. It was one of those whisper, whisper things you hear around, so I wasn't too sure until I looked up *Roselind* on the Internet. And there was a whole lot of stuff—even some old pictures of Miah at the Academy Awards. I was like, *Yo, this ain't your around the way, Brother!* And then after he died, all the stuff just started flying. I guess the cops thought it was just gonna be like, Oops, we made a mistake, but people went ballistic! Both those cops went to jail, and that's something you don't be seeing in New York—white cops going to jail for shooting a black kid— what?! Uh-uh. Most usually happens is they get desk duty until the hoopla dies down and then it's all back to how it was. The day those cops got sentenced, I swear, everybody in New York that was over the age of ten stood somewhere with their mouths hanging open. Then a whole lotta people started cheering.

Ellie was Miah's girl. They was real tight—he'd walk her to class. You'd see him in the hallway, carrying her books—sometimes she'd be carrying his books 'cause she believes in stuff like that, I guess—but still, Miah'd be looking like, *Yeah! She's mine.* It wasn't nothing snobby in it. They were in love and you could just tell it. I ain't gonna judge him. I mean, I wouldn't date no white girls, but it's just 'cause—well, for one thing, black girls got it going on, and me and my girl's tight. That interracial thing—you see it in movies and read it in books—everybody's doing that thing nowadays. But back in the day, brothers would get hung or get a serious beatdown for even looking at a white girl, so while I don't mean no disrespect to Miah, I'm not trying to forget the history. But I said *What's up?* to Ellie and she said *What's going on?* to me and we just sat there like that for a few, watching people go into the school.

"Pretty out," Ellie said.

"Yeah," I said back. "It's all right."

I took a look at Ellie's legs. Most of the girls wore their skirts real short, but hers was only kinda short and she had nice legs to go with it, even if they was mad pale.

"You're a junior this year?" Ellie asked me.

"Nah, I'm outta here. This my last year."

"You thinking about college and stuff?" Ellie looked at me. I'd never really sat this close to her. The closest I was to her was at Miah's funeral—and then I was a few rows back. I remember she wasn't crying. She sat up real straight and I remember thinking, *If somebody blinks too hard, that girl's gonna shatter like a bottle.* I tried to keep my eyes kinda open after that. Not 'cause I thought she was gonna break, really—I kept them open because I thought if *I* blinked too hard, I was gonna start crying and never be able to stop.

But now, sitting up close to Ellie, I could see that her hair wasn't just dark brown. It had some other kinds of brown in it. And when she looked at me, her eyes had some other colors in them too.

"Gonna go where the good ball teams are. That's my plan. The schools that got the good ball teams and a lotta money to shake at me. Got a couple I'm thinking about but I ain't said yes to anybody yet."

Ellie smiled.

"God, you sound just like Miah when you say—"

"You know how many times I heard that since Miah been dead?" I looked down at my backpack—too mad to look at her. "Twenty? Thirty? A hundred? Every time I turn around, somebody—and it usually ain't a black person—is saying something about me is reminding them of Miah."

"Why are you like this?" Ellie said, and I couldn't believe *she* had the nerve to be getting mad.

"Like what? Like me?"

"All angry . . . and evil." She moved her hands when she talked—like she was trying to draw who I was with those skinny pale arms.

"Guess black folks just angry people, huh? Try kicking it in my shoes, El. Some white girl dies who doesn't even look a little like you—only thing you got going on is you both white. And you one of maybe four white people at school with all black people." I looked at her, waiting for her to let what I was saying dig deep. "Say that other white girl eats some cop's bullet just 'cause she was the wrong color at the wrong time. And then people start coming out the woodwork trying to see that girl in you."

Ellie looked straight ahead and nodded.

"You know what you'd probably be thinking?" I asked then, kept going before she had a chance to answer. "You'd probably be thinking, 'Well, when the hell is MY number gonna be up?' "

"Is that what you think?"

I shrugged. "I think a whole lot of things and yeah, that's one of the thoughts. Another is—all these years gone past and white people still can't tell us apart."

"Kennedy, I was trying—"

"Doesn't matter. Think about it." A white guy passed and looked at us. When he was inside, I said, "Does *he* remind you of Miah?"

Ellie looked at me. "He doesn't play ball and he's not black—so no. And yes, I'm trying to see some Miah in you." She threw her arms out. "I'm trying to see some Miah in every single person I see—not just you. So if that makes me some kind of stupid racist, then I guess I'll be that if I get to see him a little. . . ."

I didn't say anything, just started getting my stuff together. Ellie kept looking straight ahead. Just staring.

"Yo, El. I know he was your man, and I know you guys was mad tight and all. I know it must've hurt. . . ."

"It still does," she said, real quiet.

I stood there with my backpack on my shoulder. Wasn't hardly anybody left on the stairs, and I wasn't looking to be late for math, but something kept me standing there.

"Look, El. I'm sorry I flashed on you. And I know I ain't never said this, but I'm sorry you lost your man. Miah was cool. The way I figure it, if it takes you a hundred years to get over it, then take the hundred years—it's just time, right? We all just doing our time on this planet anyways. Got a right to do it the way you need to."

Ellie looked at me for a minute. Then she nodded.

"Thanks, Kennedy."

I shrugged. "You don't have to be thanking me. I'm just telling you what's up."

I turned and started heading up the stairs. I could feel Ellie's eyes on me. And another pair of eyes too—I knew who they belonged to and I knew he was nodding and saying, *Yo, Kennedy. Thanks, man.*

Ellie

AT SCHOOL THERE WERE SIGNS EVERYWHERE—CHEERLEADING, debate team, track, soccer, chess club, reading group. I walked through the halls slowly, stopping to read each and every sign. *Come join us,* the signs seemed to beckon. *Why in God's name would anyone walk alone?*

It was true—there were kids everywhere—talking, calling to each other, sharing notes and lunch and stories about their weekends. When the bell rang, the halls got loud and busy. The sounds swirled around me and over me as I walked, as though there were some kind of invisible *thing* covering me, keeping me just that far away from everyone. How could anyone ever get it?

In the classrooms, the teachers looked at me with soft, sad eyes. In the cafeteria, I turned to catch kids whispering as they looked in my direction.

I answered questions when called on. I waved to people who waved to me. I carried my books close to my chest and walked the halls alone. The noise that was Percy Academy became muted and distant and foreign. Who were these people?

Miah died in the winter. Spring came with lots of rain. Then crocuses in patches at playgrounds, narcissus in silver pots on windows, tulips at Easter time. Then it was summer. Then it was fall again.

I remember a day with lots of snow and me not getting out of bed. I remember the morning I slammed my fist into the mirror—the glass, the bleeding, the wanting to die. But the cuts were not deep and the mirror was replaced. I remember screaming. Lots and lots of screaming. And a rage so deep, some days I couldn't stop shaking from it.

Somewhere inside of all of this, there was a funeral. There were rallies and news programs and politicians promising to protect young black men. There was a trial and two cops went to jail. Percy put up a plaque and the basketball team wore black bands around their arms.

And then there was less rage and a new hollowness. A pit of warm, dry air inside of me.

Then, for a long time, nothing at all.

Through it all, the seasons continued to change. Day

fell into night. My mother did chores. Dogs barked and car horns honked. Everywhere in the city, there were people who had no clue about the pain.

At school I took my tests. Did my homework. Each quarter, the A's on my report cards seemed to stumble over themselves. It was as if I was a grown-up coming back to school with all this new information. I had no friends. Everything and everyone seemed like it was part of a long-ago time—when I was young and free and living.

Desire Viola Roselind

ALL DAY LONG, THE CICADAS BEAT THEIR WINGS. THE SUN moves out from behind clouds and shines on your skin. I sit, fanning myself, a tall glass of lemonade always at my side. You want summer—it's summer. You want to watch the leaves change color, you move to another spot and you got yourself some autumn. Or maybe you feel like lying on the ground and making yourself a snow angel— just take some steps and you got yourself your own private winter. My grandson won't go near the snow. He says it reminds him of the night he fell. He won't say *died*.

I sit in my big chair and watch him watching the world some days. His body sags down and he lets himself get all wrapped up in a sadness just like his daddy used to do. I look at him and see Norman and Nelia and my own daddy—all coming through to him.

Jeremiah, you don't always got to be watching the

world, I say. I'm sitting in my spring with the cicadas singing. Jeremiah sitting in summer with the heat coming down and the sun so bright, the sky where he is is near white.

Jeremiah has a basketball. He can hold it in one hand. He can shoot it from way over there and it goes right into the basket. He can bounce it all kinds of ways that make you believe in magic. If he wants to play some basketball, all he's gotta do is get up and walk on over there and some boys who play really good will show up and they'll have themselves a good game. He gets the ball in the basket a whole lot of times. And he can do some fancy moves to take it away from one of the other boys.

That's when you see Jeremiah grinning.

But most days he just sits and watches the world. And that's when I try to talk to him.

You done left that world behind you, I say. *Let it go.*

But Jeremiah looks out on the world and shakes his head.

Can't let it go, Grandma. Got too many people missing me. Thinking about me. And I'm thinking about them too.

I look out at my flowers. The roses are red and pink and striped. Got roses with different-colored petals on the same flowers. Purple roses with color so deep, you choke up looking at them. Yellow-orange ones like little flames coming out of the green. Tulips too. And corn high as Jeremiah's head already and the spring still new. Got some rhubarb. Might bake a pie just to feel the crust forming against the palms of my hands. When my garden needs rain, it rains. Oh, if only living could've been like this.

If Jeremiah wanted, he could be in the front row of his favorite ball team's game. He could be swimming or eating ice cream. He could know what it feels like to fly. If he were a different kind of boy, he could stand in fire just because it was something he'd always wanted to do, or take steps down into the ocean and touch some shark's fin. Braid up the tentacles of a jellyfish.

But he's not that kind of boy. He's just a boy who can't let the world that he left behind get behind him.

I lean forward a little bit in my chair. I touch his head. Those twists he got is something I don't understand, but I still think his hair is beautiful. All of him is my beautiful Jeremiah. I let my hand run along his head and stare out to see what he's staring out at. There's his mama and daddy—Norman looking like he's putting on a little weight. I see Jeremiah's girl, Elisha, and her peoples. I see some animals, some little children, a ball game at Jeremiah's school. He's watching so many people and so many things.

One day, I say, *each of them is gonna be on this side with you. Seems like it's gonna take forever—*

I wish—

No you don't.

Jeremiah is sitting cross-legged at my feet. He's got the ball in his lap. Now he lowers his head until his forehead is touching it.

Yeah, Grandma. I do.

You left that world and it closed up behind you, Jeremiah. The way water do when a body climbs out of it. First there's some ripples and then the water gets all still again.

Jeremiah lifts his head up and lets himself smile a little. *The water's still rippling, though.*

I look out to where he's looking and I see he's telling the truth.

Ellie

NELIA WAS SITTING ON THE STOOP WHEN I GOT THERE EARLY
Saturday afternoon. She was wearing an orange T-shirt
and a beautiful tie-dyed skirt that wrapped around her
waist a couple of times and came all the way down to her
ankles. I walked down the block slowly, watching her as
she wrote in a black binder that covered a lot of her lap.
The block was quiet. At the other end, a group of girls
were playing hand games. I tried to listen to the song they
were singing, but they were singing so fast, the words
blurred together. Nelia'd gotten thin over the months. Her
face looked smaller, the cheekbones jumping up from it in
a way that was at once beautiful and alarming. I grabbed
the strap of my shoulder bag, needing something—anything—to hold on to. She would always be Miah's mom
to me.

"Hey, Nelia," I said when I was still a few feet away from her.

Nelia looked up, surprised. Then, slowly, she smiled. Miah's smile. I stood there for a moment, not able to take another step.

Then Nelia said, "I was hoping you'd stop by." And I felt myself melting, moving toward her like she was a life raft or something. We hugged and she held me tightly. I could feel her ribs beneath her shirt and skin, feel her still smiling.

"Sit down." She motioned to the stoop and I sat down one stair below her. For some reason the idea of sitting on the same step seemed too much. I needed to be able to look up at her.

"What are you working on? I mean—is it okay to ask that?"

Nelia gave me a puzzled look, then nodded. "Of course." She closed the binder. "I wish I could answer it, though—I don't really know. Just thoughts. Lots and lots of thoughts."

"Oh."

She touched my hair. Her hand felt so unfamiliar and so familiar at the same time.

"It's the way the books come to me. Thoughts are a good thing. A beginning."

Before I knew Miah, before I knew Nelia, I'd had to read a novel of hers for English class. It was about a black woman who was a civil rights attorney. She went back south to visit family and ended up in slavery. The teacher kept calling it magical realism, but there was nothing magical about it to me—It was one of the scariest, most impactful books I'd ever read. It haunted me for ages afterward. When the class discussed it, I couldn't even say anything and I remember the teacher asking if I had read it. It's strange. I'd read it the year before I'd met Miah. Then there he was in my life. Then there was Nelia Roselind, author of *And Back Again*. Who would have known they were heading toward my life? Who could have told me? What would I have believed? If someone had said, *You're going to meet the son of this author—a black guy, Ellie—you're going to fall in love with him and then he's going to die,* I would have backed away from that person. I would have given them such a look and called them crazy.

I leaned back against the step and stared up at the sky. Nelia and I were quiet for a while. It was beautiful out— the leaves were just beginning to change and there was only the slightest bit of wind, a strange wind, like someone stroking my shoulders.

Nelia put the binder down on the step beside her. It had

been a long time since she had written—I knew that. And I knew why too.

"It's been a long time," Nelia said. She smiled at me and I knew it was because my face showed everything. Surprise. Embarrassment. "You were just thinking that, weren't you?"

I nodded.

"Since Norman and I—"

"Broke up." I looked down at my fingers. "He left you—for Lois Ann King." The words came quickly. It felt like I had said them a thousand times. But I hadn't. Only heard it—again and again from Miah. *It busted my mama's heart wide open,* Miah used to say. *Hasn't written anything since.*

Nelia frowned. "Your life gets away from you," she said. "The older you get, the less of it you own."

I didn't understand what she was talking about, but she kept talking and it seemed that it didn't matter, right then, whether or not I was there.

"Even you knowing the whole story—whether I wanted you to or not—"

"I'm sorry—"

"No. It's not a secret anymore. We would've gotten close and eventually you would've known. But the fact that you knew the whole story before you even knew me—that part. That's your life not being your own any-more. It's funny. It's like writing a book—once it's out there, people say and do whatever they want with it. You have no control."

She looked at me, frowning still. "But who has control over *anything*, right?"

We were both quiet for a while. The sun went behind some clouds and everything got a bit darker for a moment. Then the sun came out again.

Nelia said, "It's hard to write when there's so much drama in your own life. Your own life gets in the way." She let out a long breath and looked down the block. The girls were still doing their hand-clapping thing and she watched them for a minute. "That's an old one—*Down, down, baby, down by the roller coaster, sweet, sweet baby, I'll never letcha go. Jimmy Jimmy coco-pop. Jimmy Jimmy pop!*"

I laughed. "Is that what they're saying?"

Nelia rolled her eyes. "Over and over and over. Some-one needs to teach them something new. If they keep it up, it's going to be the title of this book. *Down, Down, Baby, Down by the Roller Coaster, Sweet, Sweet Baby, I Will Never Let You Go* by Nelia Roselind."

We laughed.

"And you'd probably get a Pulitzer for it."

"Oh, please, no. Who wants that much attention?"

"We read a book of yours in English Lit last year. And when I first got to Percy, we read *And Back Again*."

Nelia raised an eyebrow. "Really? I'd think that was a little young to be reading that book."

I shrugged. "It was for a Women's Lit class—I think it was mostly older kids taking the course. I thought the book was really beautiful—and really scary."

Nelia smiled. "I couldn't even imagine." She looked out over the block and shivered a little, then rubbed her hands over her arms. "When I'm writing, really in the heart of writing—it's like I'm not even there. Sarahbeth . . . you know, the main character . . ."

I nodded.

"She was so . . . so *foreign* to me. And every time something unexpected happened, I had to put my pen down . . . and shake it off. I couldn't *imagine* reading that book. Writing it was enough for me."

"But . . . I mean, then where does the stuff . . . the stuff you write about come from?"

Nelia shrugged. "I don't know really. I just write it down and ask no questions."

We looked at each other without saying anything. The girls had finally stopped singing and now there was piano music coming from one of the buildings across the street. Then, after a moment, a guy's voice, singing. I recognized the song—an old one by Fleetwood Mac. My sisters, who are both way older than me, used to listen to it all the time. It was a beautiful song about things changing.

"He has such a stunning voice," Nelia said.

We sat there listening awhile. The song made me think of so many things—of Anne and her girlfriend living in San Francisco. Of school and the kids who couldn't understand why the missing still hurt. Just last week, I'd overheard some girls talking in the hallway at school—maybe they had meant for me to hear, I don't know. *She's such a widow,* one of them said. *Give me a break, he was her boyfriend for less than a year. Get over it already.* I'd kept walking, ignoring them. Bounce back. Move on. Hide your tears. Get over it. That's how the world seemed to work. We get an hour to grieve, a few days off from school or work, then we're supposed to be right back in the world, as good as anything. I looked over toward the music and closed my eyes, blinking back the stupid tears that were welling up in them. That's why I was here—sitting on Nelia's stoop, close enough to touch her. I needed someone who understood that the hurting doesn't just stop, that the absence is so much bigger, so much more painful, so much more *present* than the presence was.

"Do you know who's singing?" I asked.

"That's Carlton. Miah's friend. You must have met him."

I smiled, remembering him. "I met him a few times. He was sweet. And funny."

We sat there, listening. His voice was amazing—soft and lilting. There was such a sadness to it. The Carlton I'd met hadn't had that sadness to him. But none of us did—not back then. Not before . . .

"You should go see him," Nelia said. "You're right—he is sweet." After a moment, almost to herself, she said, "Sweet and sad."

She picked up her binder again, opened it. "Number 434. Just ring the bell at the top of the stairs."

I stood up and she pointed across the street. "That brownstone over there. Follow the music." She smiled, then hugged me again, picked up her pen and leaned into the pages.

Jeremiah

WHEN I SIT DOWN BESIDE MY MOTHER, SHE SHIVERS. WHEN I touch Ellie's shoulders, she smiles like she knows it's me. Maybe she does. Who could have told me that the wind was some passed-on soul stopping to touch your face, your hands, your hair. Who knew a surprising cool breeze was someone who had gone before you, saying, "You're loved."

You're loved, Mama.

Ellie . . . you're loved.

Some days I wish hard for the chance to kiss Ellie again. But today—this moment—the two of them sitting on the stoop is perfect.

This is what I know now: In your life there will be perfect moments. And in your afterlife too.

My grandmother watches me and shakes her head. *Leave the living alone,* she says. But she doesn't understand. It's not easy to let go. Even if you turn your back on the world you left, you're still pulled toward it, you're still turning around—always—to look behind you. To make sure everyone's okay.

Carlton

SATURDAY MORNING, I WENT OVER TO A PICKUP GAME AT FORT Greene Park. I knew some of the brothers playing, but a bunch of them had come over from Bed-Stuy and Brownsville. One brother had on a Percy shirt. He had pretty good game, so I decided to ask him.

"What do you know about Percy?" I said.

He looked me up and down. Not in a mean way, but more in a *Who the hell is this light-skinned brother?* way. I'd seen the look a lot from darker-skinned brothers. It was a "chump until proven un-chump" look. I kept my gaze steady.

"What *you* know about it?" he asked back.

"I know they should have slammed Dalton in their final game last year, but didn't."

"True that." Then he let himself grin a little and held up his hand. I slapped it.

"Kennedy," he said. "I play ball there."

"Carlton. I'm over here at Tech."

The other guys were standing around the basket, tossing the ball around and taking shots. Me and Kennedy were standing midcourt. He was tall, about my height. I noticed right away that anytime he wasn't smiling, he was frowning.

Someone tossed him the ball and he took a shot— hardly even turning to look at the basket. The ball went in, though—nice and smooth too.

"I got Kennedy," I said. We were choosing up sides, and seeing his jump, I knew I wanted him on my team.

"I seen you play," Kennedy said. "You play a'ight." He smiled again. I looked back over to the other guys and picked another one. It went back and forth like that for a minute.

"You know Miah?" I asked Kennedy.

He'd bent down to pull up the tongue in his sneakers, but he stopped midpull and looked up at me. "Who ain't know Miah? After he got shot, everybody in New York claimed a piece of him."

"Yeah," I said.

Kennedy kept on looking at me. "He lived around here, didn't he?"

"On my block." I didn't look at him, just kept picking guys until each team had five players. "We went way back." After a minute I said, "Grew up together. Knew him since we were both five or six. He was my boy."

"So you really knew him—not just fronting like a lot of people."

"Yeah. We were pretty tight."

"The cops messed up. Nothing new, though," Kennedy said. "I didn't know him tight like you did, but he was always cool with me."

"Miah ain't all gone. He's still here."

Kennedy looked at me. And I looked back at him.

"You don't feel him?" I said.

He stared at me for another minute, then shrugged. "You know," he said. "Whatever."

"Check it," somebody said, and we started throwing the ball around. I took a shot and missed it. Kennedy retrieved the ball and chucked it back to me. We were just playing around, hadn't started a real game yet.

I dribbled the ball through my legs and behind my back, shot it and watched it sail in.

"Let's stop playing around and get this game on," one of the guys said.

I nodded. "Hit or miss, yo," I said.

Kennedy held his hands out. I threw him the ball and he took the shot, a sweet sinker. The game was on.

By the time I got home, it was late in the afternoon and I was sweaty and hungry as anything. The house was empty. My mom had cleaned and the hardwood floors smelled like the oil soap she used to clean them with. I made myself some lunch and ate it standing at the kitchen counter. I smelled bad and could feel myself stinking up my mother's clean kitchen, so I finished eating and went upstairs to take a shower. The whole time the water was washing away the funk, I was thinking about Kennedy—not only about the great game of ball he had going on, but also about the way he looked at me when I said that thing about Miah still being with us. There was something in that look that let me know that he felt it too. His look kept flashing in my head and then disappearing and replacing itself with how beautiful all those guys looked running up and down the court. I turned the water to cold, wanting to shut it all out. I didn't want to think about anything—not about Miah, not about Kennedy, not about the beautiful bodies of ballplayers . . .

After I got dressed, I went back downstairs and sat at the piano. The windows were wide-open—whenever my moms cleaned, she did that—like she was hoping the whole block could see what a clean house we had. I smiled and shook my head, not bothering to close them. That song "Landslide" had come to me again—all the words—and I tapped a few keys, ready to play it. I sang the song softly at first, letting the words move through me. I could feel myself beginning to sing louder and louder, wanting to forget, to sing right over the part of the day that made me feel ashamed—thinking about those beautiful bodies. And remember the good stuff—scoring, Kennedy's look, our team winning by ten points. Maybe I had sung the song twice or three times when the doorbell rang.

I waited a minute, hoping whoever it was would go away. But they didn't. The bell rang again and I figured I might as well answer it.

At first I didn't know who she was. She'd changed over the months. Her hair was longer and her clothes seemed—different. Then I remembered I'd only seen her out of her uniform once and that was at Miah's funeral. That day, she was dressed in black like everyone else. But this time, she was wearing jeans—the kind that fit low on the hips in a way that looked nice on her. She looked paler than I remembered. For some reason I'd remembered her as being the same complexion as my mom, but she wasn't. Her skin was whiter. The kind of skin that burned right up in the sun. Then she smiled. And I remembered that smile, remembered the way Miah always grinned when he talked about it.

"Hey, Ellie," I said.

She looked surprised. Then her smile got bigger. "So you remember me?"

I stepped back and let her in. "How am I gonna forget the love of my best friend's life?"

Ellie looked at me. "Is that what he called me?"

"He called you a lot of things."

"I heard you singing."

"Yeah. I sing."

We stood in the foyer a minute without saying anything, just sort of looking at each other. It was starting to get dark out and the inside of the house seemed too dark.

"I was visiting Nelia," Ellie said. "She showed me where you lived. Thought I'd, you know, stop by and say hey."

"Hey yourself. It's nice to see you." I put my hands in my pockets, then took them out again. "Come in," I said, backing up a bit. "You want some water or juice or something?"

Ellie shook her head, looking around as she walked, taking everything in, I guess. Our house was full of art that my dad collected—African masks, drums, oil paintings, things like that. She walked over to the couch and sat on the edge of it.

"It's pretty here."

"Yeah," I said. "It's a nice place. Lived here most of my life. You're uptown, right?"

She nodded. "Central Park West. An apartment—not a house. Brooklyn makes me wish we lived in a house, though. So much more air."

"Sometimes it's a lot of hot air, though. People hanging out, talking junk. I love Brooklyn, though. It's home to me."

We got quiet again. I didn't have any idea what else to say to her. She was Miah's girl and now Miah was gone. In some fairy-tale type novel, she'd probably end up being my girl, but this wasn't that kind of story. She was pretty enough and all, though. Maybe Kennedy . . .

"Hey—do you know this guy Kennedy? He goes to your school?"

A small frown, and then she said, "Yeah—I know him somewhat. He's not very friendly."

"It's New York," I said. "Who is?"

She nodded. "That's true. How come you ask? You know him?"

"He was over this way, playing ball in the park today. He's got good game. That was the first time I met him, though. Miah'd talked about his game a couple of times and I'd seen him play."

Ellie nodded. "He's supposed to be pretty smart too. I tried to talk to him a couple of times, but—he pretty much brushed me off." She shrugged. "I think it was my fault, though. I said something about him sounding like Miah. Sounds like, from what he said, he hears that a lot."

"You know how people are. He was probably getting

compared to Miah right and left. Especially at a place like Percy."

"Yeah. He kind of suggested that was the case." She looked across the living room. The windows go from the ceiling to the floor almost. I watched her staring out at the block. It was almost dark now. "I don't know. I was just trying to make conversation."

I got up and went into the kitchen and took two bottles of water from the fridge, then came back and tossed one to her. "Why?"

"Why what?"

"Why *try* to make conversation . . . why *try* to make it with Kennedy? Either convo happens or it doesn't."

Ellie opened the bottle of water and took a sip. "To connect. To remember. To forget. All of the above. Wrong reasons and right reasons."

"Yeah, I hear you. I get it."

"You know . . . ," Ellie said softly, "I feel like the world stopped. And I got off . . . and then it started spinning again, but too fast for me to hop back on. I feel like I'm still trying to get a . . . to get some kind of foothold on living."

I raised an eyebrow. "That's deep."

"You don't feel that way? I mean—you guys were best friends."

"Yeah. But for me, it's like there's this place where

84

there's just . . . nothing. Like this hole or something. I throw some TV or a movie or a book in it every now and then. I throw a lot of ball in there, and music—you know, I take steps. Press on."

Ellie stared out the window, then sighed and leaned back into the couch. "I guess that's what we're doing, huh? Guess we're pressing on."

"Yep."

"No girlfriend, huh?"

"Nope."

She looked at me. Then without blinking she said, "Boyfriend?"

"Nah. Just me. Just me trying to figure it all out." It felt like something heavy lifted up off of me. I took a breath and the breath came easily. Ellie hadn't even *blinked.*

"I think the figuring out takes forever," she said. "It seems like everybody's trying to figure something out."

"How about you—what's your thing? The thing you're trying to figure out? I mean, besides how to hop back onto the world."

Ellie shrugged. "I don't know, really—I mean, I guess that's the thing. How do we go on? How do we get back on the world and move along?"

"Well . . ." I sat down on the couch beside her. "I guess this is a step, huh? You ringing my bell."

Ellie smiled again. "I guess."

"It's a big day for me," I said.

" 'Cause I rang your bell?"

I took another sip of water. She hadn't even *blinked* when she asked about a boyfriend. And here I was thinking there'd be the world exploding out from under me.

"Yeah," I said. "Glad you crossed that street and rang my bell."

"Well, then I guess I'll have to do it again sometime."

"You better."

"And maybe one day you can cross that bridge to Manhattan."

"Maybe—it's a long bridge."

Ellie nudged me with her shoulder and smiled. I nudged her back.

"Nah, really, though," I said. "Thanks."

"Don't thank me. Nelia's the one who pointed your house out and suggested I come say hi. I just followed the music."

I started singing the song again. Ellie listened and after a moment she joined in—her voice high and soft in a way that blended nicely. I was surprised she knew the words, but didn't stop to ask her about it.

"And I saw my reflection . . . "

When the song ended, we sat there drinking our water and staring outside. It grew dark, but I didn't turn on any lights. Somewhere someone was playing a Stevie Wonder tune. Somewhere else, a little kid was singing her ABC's. Then the block got quiet. And another day was almost over.

Kennedy

SUNDAY, MY MOMS WAKES ME UP EARLY AND I TAKE A SHOWER, grease my braids a little and put on some decent clothes. She's already dressed, wearing dark blue, her black coat and pocketbook on the couch next to her Bible.

"Made you some bacon and eggs," she says when I come out of the bathroom. She sets the plate down on the kitchen table and smiles at me. "Don't you look nice."

I smile back, sit down and say, "So do you."

Sunday mornings, I miss my dad the most. His chair across from mine is empty. In our building some of the kids got dads and some don't. Some of them never met their dads and some see them on weekends.

Sunday mornings, we go to church and then go see my dad.

The whole time the preacher's preaching, I'm thinking about my dad. If anybody asked, I'd say he was good—like in his heart, he was good. You'd see him coming down the street and he was always carrying some lady's bag or helping somebody with one of their kids or giving some poor chump some spare change. That's the kind of guy I remember him being—somebody who was always thinking about other people. I guess somebody like that should have gone out real tragic—like, shot or something—like Miah. But he didn't. He went out early because he had a whacked heart. Something from when he was young that just stayed on and caught him when he was thirty-seven. Makes you always think about how you're living.

Even though it's freezing, the cemetery is hopping. Sunday seems to be Visit the Dead Day—people walking slowly up and down the rows and rows of dead people or crouching all close around some tiny grave. Makes a body wonder if the dead know what Sunday is and get all ready.

My daddy's grave is in a lot about a quarter mile in then another twenty feet to the left. KENNEDY MAYARD SR. it says. Something about the way his name looks there makes me wish gravestones wasn't stone—it seems real permanent that way. Like it's saying, *You better believe he's dead!*

I make a fist and pound it against my heart a couple of times, then throw the peace sign at him. My moms fixes the plastic flowers around the gravestone. We stand there a little while without saying anything. Then I'm feeling my dad right there with us—his arm around my mom's shoulder, his big hand rubbing my head.

My moms pulls her coat tighter and says, "Sure is windy today, isn't it?"

I look out over the cemetery. Even though it's only the third day of November, I see the first few flakes of snow.

Me and my moms stand there watching it come down—all soft and slow and cold.

It's strange the way death connects people. I wasn't real tight with Miah when he was living, but now here I was, standing in a brick-cold cemetery, feeling my dad everywhere and knowing that me and Ellie and Miah's moms and pops and everybody who'd ever lost somebody they'd been tight with—we all . . . it was like, I don't know—like a continuum—and we're all a part of the same something. We ate our breakfast and did our work and had conversations that were stupid and conversations that weren't so stupid. At night we closed our eyes and hoped sleep came quickfast. And with all of our living going on, our dead peeps were there—everywhere. Watching over us, holding us up, giving us some kinda reasons for going to church and school and the basketball courts. Always right there, making sure we kept on keeping on. I guess if anybody asked, I'd tell them we were all doing what the living do.

I take my mom's hand, pull her a little bit closer to me. She smells like cold weather and perfume.

"Your daddy always liked himself some snow," my moms says.

And we stand there, freezing our behinds off and watching it fall.

Norman Roselind

WHEN I FIRST MOVED TO FORT GREENE, WHAT I LOVED MOST were the trees. The city had planted saplings back in the sixties and now the trees stand like soldiers up and down the block. As though they're guarding the residents of Fort Greene from harm. I wish I could say they do. It amazes me that they're still standing—that anyone or anything is still standing. The trees change—leaves bud, grow green and wide, wither, turn red and brown, then fall. Again and again. Year after year. When Miah was a little boy, he'd climb up and swing on the lowest branches and invariably, some adult would lean out of a window and say, "Miah, get down off of that tree and let it grow like you grow." For some reason, that always made Miah laugh—the idea of a tree having the same upward journey as himself.

Some mornings, I sit on my stoop and look at the *Times*, see the way the world is stopping and the way it just keeps moving on. Amazing how it keeps moving on. Amazing how people can melt themselves into each new day.

This morning, Nelia was sitting across the street on her stoop. Used to be our stoop.

The wind was blowing hard. It'd been cold last night and the day felt like it was trying to warm up but not doing a good job at it. Nelia was leaning over her writing. Her hair was getting longer and it sort of fell down a bit over her face in a way I'd never seen it do. Miah's death had added some years to her and thinned her up. At some angles she looked like the Vassar girl I'd fallen in love with years and years ago. Then she looked like an older, more beautiful version of the woman I'd walked away from. I closed my eyes. Miah'd never understood how two people could stop loving each other and I'd never known how to explain.

After a while of watching Nelia, I took a deep breath, folded the paper under my arm, got up from my stoop and crossed the street.

How many years had it been since I'd crossed that street—three, four, nine? Even after Miah died, I still didn't go back into that house. I'd offered to help clean out his room, but Nelia had said no, said she'd take care of it. Now here were my feet, one stepping in front of the other, and me moving closer and closer to Nelia's stoop.

The block is silent as a stone. It feels like somebody far away is watching. And waiting to see what happens.

Ellie

EARLY SATURDAY MORNING, MARION SHAKES ME AWAKE. MY throat hurts and I'm not sure where I am.

"You were screaming," she says.

I blink, look around my room.

"Someone shot Miah," I whisper, pressing my hand to my throat. "I dreamed someone shot Miah."

Marion stares at me and shakes her head. She leaves and a few minutes later, she's back, pressing a warm cloth to my forehead.

"I dreamed . . ."

"Shhhh, Elisha," she whispers. "Miah's gone, honey."

I lay back on the bed and close my eyes. "Miah's gone," I whisper, sinking back into sleep.

When I came downstairs later, I was surprised to find my father sitting at the kitchen table. The apartment smelled like cinnamon, apples and coffee. Marion gave me a long look, then put a glass of juice on the table in front of me.

"What are you doing home?" I asked my father. He was usually at the hospital on Saturdays. Sundays were our day together.

"Your mother tells me you had another bad dream," my father said. He looked tired, his blue eyes were rimmed and puffy. My sisters and brother call me "the accident" because I was born ten years after the last one. My parents aren't young. Last year, we celebrated my mother's fifty-seventh birthday.

I looked at Marion. "And?"

"And we're worried," she said. "It's been almost a year now, Elisha."

"It's been eleven months, *Marion*."

"Don't call your mother 'Marion,' El."

I pushed the juice away from me. "When she starts calling me 'Ellie,' I'll start calling her 'Mom'—"

"Your name is Elisha." Marion turned back to the stove and stirred something. After a moment, she set a bowl of apple compote on the table, then took a stack of pancakes from the oven.

I got up and poured myself some coffee.

"We're just concerned," my father said. "You don't participate in school—"

"I get straight A's." I tried to keep my voice even.

"You don't do any activities, just study, study, study," Marion said. She sat across from me and put two pancakes on a plate. "Here."

"Not hungry."

My father looked at me and I rolled my eyes and took the plate from Marion.

"No sports, no clubs, no friends . . . ," Marion said, counting off on her fingers. "Just bad dreams and sadness. Just you in your room, doing I don't know what. . . ."

"*Studying*. I'm *studying* in my room. And I do other stuff besides hang out upstairs."

"Like what?" Marion and my father looked at me. "Where are your friends? Girls your age are supposed to have lots of girlfriends hanging around and calling. Nobody ever calls here for you. When the other kids were home, the phone was constantly—"

"Well, I'm not *the other kids*. You should have stopped when you were ahead if you wanted *the other kids*."

"We were thinking," my father said, "that maybe you want to talk to somebody—"

I started to say something, but he put his hand up.

"I know we've talked about it before, but now all this time has passed and you're the same."

I'm not the same, I wanted to scream. *I'm different. My boyfriend was killed. That does something to a person.*

"Sometimes I go to Brooklyn and visit Miah's mother

97

and Carlton," I said. I knew I couldn't make them understand, and I knew some psychiatrist friend of my father's wouldn't understand either.

"When are you taking all these trips to Brooklyn?" Marion asked.

"Just sometimes." I took a bite of pancake and chewed slowly.

Both of them waited.

"Who's Carlton?" Marion wanted to know.

I looked up at the clock over the kitchen sink. It was almost nine thirty. Carlton and I had said we'd meet downtown at eleven for brunch.

"He was Miah's best friend."

My mother put her fork down on the table. "And now you're dating *him*?"

"God—can't you guys leave me alone? I'm not *dating* him."

"What's going on, Ellie?" my father said. "What's this about? There're plenty of boys living right around you. Nice boys."

"You mean *white* boys, Dad."

"I mean more appropriate boys." My father looked at me and I looked back at him without saying anything. I'd always loved him more than my mother and maybe that's why it hurt to hear him talk like that.

"Give me a break, Dad. Cut the liberal crap. You mean white boys, but you would never say that, because it would be politically incorrect, wouldn't it?"

My father shook his head and stared at me like he was trying to figure out who I was.

Marion got up and went over to the sink. She stood there with her back to us as though she'd forgotten what she'd gone there for.

"Maybe it's a good thing, honey. Maybe it means less sadness in the house."

"I don't understand you," my father said. "I thought I did, but I don't."

"I understand *you* even less," I said. "And I'm not dating him. He's . . . he's a friend."

"Well," Marion said. "It's good to hear you're making some friends. I don't want you going all the way to Brooklyn, though."

"I'm meeting him downtown today." I took another bite of pancake. "Don't worry—I won't be crossing that dangerous bridge into an outer borough."

"Don't be sarcastic," my father said. "I still think we need to talk about you seeing someone."

I stood up. "How about family therapy? I'm game for that. How about I get a chance to talk about why I was too scared to bring my black boyfriend home to parents who swear they're not racist. How about we talk about him dying without you ever meeting him because somewhere along the way, I got the message that it wasn't okay—"

"Bring this new friend home," Marion said. "No one's stopping you."

I didn't take my eyes off my father. "That's not the point, is it?"

"It's all something we need to talk about," he said.

I shook my head. "We never will," I said.

My parents were silent. They knew it was true.

Carlton

"IT'S FUNNY. THERE'S THIS PART OF ME THAT ALWAYS KINDA felt alone, you know?"

We're in a coffee shop on the corner of Waverly and Sixth Avenue. There are people all around us—men and men together, women and men, parents and kids, women and women.

"I used to come here with Miah," Ellie said, leading me to a table in the back. We sat down and a waiter put two menus in front of us. The place was quieter than it seemed it ought to be. I looked up and saw that the ceilings were covered with a purple foamy material that must have absorbed a lot of the sound.

"How'd you guys find it—I mean, I come to the Village a lot and I never even noticed this place."

Ellie looked at me. "We were walking once. God, it all feels like such a long time ago. And we passed this couple—interracial—older, like in their thirties or something. And the guy says to Miah, 'Yo, take your honey . . .' and he told us about this place. We just smiled. It was like this bonding moment or something. And then we came here. All kinds of people mixed up all kinds of ways. Black, white, gay, straight. It doesn't make any kind of difference here."

I looked around, nodding. It was easy to imagine Miah here with Ellie, the two of them at a quiet table, drinking cappuccinos and talking about their lives. Nobody looking at them, judging them, hating them just because . . .

I stared down at the menu, my eyes starting to burn. Maybe it was the big memory of Miah. Maybe it was thinking about how good that must have felt, to be out and open and not caring about the rest of the world. When the waiter returned, we both ordered and I started messing with a napkin, tearing it into tiny pieces. I couldn't look at Ellie for some reason. The word *gay* seemed so loud, so everywhere at once.

"Something about coming here," Ellie said. "It made me so sure of Miah. So sure that I loved him. That everything would be okay." Her voice cracked a bit and she got quiet again.

Outside, snow was blowing—not a whole lot, and it probably wouldn't stick, but enough to let us know that winter was definitely here.

"You're lucky," I said. "I mean, to have had a chance to feel so sure about something. There's not one single part of me I've ever been a hundred percent sure about."

"Hmmm." Ellie looked at me. "Nothing?"

"Ball, I guess. I wasn't always sure of my game, but I always loved playing ball." I opened my palm and stared at it. "The way the ball feels in my hand. The way a shot slides into a basket. Running full court and getting underneath the backboard in time—all of that's always felt . . . felt real. Solid. But show me a ballplayer that's out there going pro saying, 'My boyfriend Bob and me . . .' "

Ellie smiled. Our food came.

"Don't exist," I said after the waiter left. "I don't exist."

"I thought you said you didn't have a boyfriend?" Ellie looked at me, frowning.

"I *don't*. That's what I'm saying. I don't exist—gay ballplayers don't exist."

"That's crazy, Carlton. You're going to stop being who you are because—"

"Yep."

"But that's not . . . that's not *living*."

"I know."

"And just because people aren't *out*, doesn't mean they don't exist."

I didn't say anything. If someone had said to me, *Carlton, are you straight or gay? Tell me now because you*

103

might be dead tomorrow, I would say, *I'm gay*—even though I've never kissed another guy or been in love with anybody.

"I *am* gay," I said, not looking at Ellie. I watched the syrup sink into my pancakes, watched the way the orange slices beside the pancakes lay still as glass.

"I know," Ellie said.

When I looked up, she was smiling again.

We stared at each other for a long time. I felt myself choking up. Felt like Ellie had just saved my life somehow. I wanted to holler, to reach across the table and lift her up. But my breath was coming too fast and my body felt heavy and light all at once, so I just sat there, staring at her.

"We'd make a nice couple—aesthetically, don't you think?" Ellie said.

I laughed and the air felt the tiniest bit lighter.

"Seriously, Carlton. You're beautiful—you could have guys dropping for you all over the place."

I took a bite of my pancakes, shook my head.

"I think I'm some kind of romantic. I would love to fall in love and feel like that's it—that's the be-all, end-all, forever amen."

Ellie's fork froze. When she looked at me, I don't know if I was surprised to see her eyes were watery. She blinked but didn't say anything.

"I know that's what you guys had," I said quickly.

"I just wonder . . . you know—if you can have it more than once. I mean, I'm not looking and I don't know if I'll ever be looking. I wasn't even looking when I found Miah." She laughed. "But . . . who knows. Who knows anything."

"I can't even imagine your world."

Ellie smiled.

"Yeah," she said. "That's what I like—you don't even try to."

"Miah loved you like crazy—you know that, right?"

Ellie stared down at her plate and nodded. "Most days," she said.

"All days."

"Most days I know it was all days. But some days . . ." She looked up at me and laughed a little bit. "Some days, I think—"

"Well, those days you're wrong."

"I know. I mean, most of me knows."

"Your food's getting cold."

She started eating. I watched her for a while.

"It never even crossed my mind to go uptown and see you," I said. "But I'm sure as hell glad you crossed that street."

"Like I said before, don't thank me—thank Nelia."

I started eating again. "You. Nelia. Whoever. I'm glad it happened."

"Yeah." Ellie looked over at me and smiled. Miah was right—it was one of the prettiest smiles I'd ever seen— real, deep, sincere, like her face and heart were wide-open.

"You want to catch a movie later?"

Ellie nodded. "Definitely."

"We'll get the paper and see what's playing, cool?"

"Way cool with me."

It was Saturday morning still. The rest of the day was ours. The rest of our life was ours. Winter was coming and it was cold outside. But we were sitting inside a restaurant that was quiet and warm. The food was good. The company was good. Maybe one day I'd have myself someone to be in love with. But even if I didn't right now, the world was ours. And here me and Ellie were, sitting across from each other. Smiling.

Kennedy

IN THE SECOND QUARTER, TRINITY SNATCHES THE BALL FROM our weak point guard—who should be sitting on the bench, but isn't because his daddy gives big money to Percy—and scores. I curse and the ref calls a foul on me because you ain't supposed to be cursing on the court. Our team's down by ten points and looking to lose yet another game. It's my third foul, so the coach pulls me off the floor. I curse again, but not so anybody can hear it, take the bench, feeling the sweat rolling off me, and put the towel over my head so I can't see how bad we're doing.

"Gotta learn to watch that mouth, Kennedy," the coach says to me.

"Yeah, whatever," I say from under the towel.

"And that attitude."

I don't say *whatever* again, but I'm thinking it hard enough for the whole gym to feel it. It's full tonight because this game is only the fourth one in the season and even though we already lost the first two out of three, people still feeling hopeful about Percy. I hear the crowd cheering and look out from underneath my towel to see Percy score from midcourt. Even more surprised to see that it's our weak point guard actually doing something for the team.

The game goes back and forth for a while and I don't look at the coach because I don't want him to see how much I'm hurting to get back in the game.

"Keep yourself warm," Coach says, throwing me my sweats. "No use cramping up."

I pull the sweats on. Percy scores two more baskets and then gets fouled. After a while the score's tied.

"Go on out," Coach says to me. He pulls the point guard out and we slap hands on the way on and off the court. His hand is sweaty and he's got this big grin on his face like he's done a whole lot.

The crowd starts cheering when they see I'm back. Since Miah's been gone, I'm the big scorer on the team. He'd get out here and pull down twenty, thirty, sometimes even forty points a game. Most games, I go home with about twenty. Coach says if my attitude was a little better, I'd probably pull down a whole lot more.

It's Percy's ball and the forward shoots it my way. I

take it up court and slip a layout in easily. The crowd starts going crazy, cheering and stomping and whistling. Even though I'm still bent about that foul, I feel myself starting to grin. I flip the crowd a peace sign and they go even crazier.

We score a few more baskets and then even *I'm* feeling the love in the room. I look over at Coach and he's got this big smile on his face. Like he's thinking what I'm thinking—*Hey, y'all—we're the Percy Panthers. And we're BACK!*

Outside, there's like a trillion stars in the sky and the night's colder than anything. I pull my hood over my head and lift my knapsack higher on my shoulder, ready to make a quick trek to the subway, when I hear somebody calling my name. I turn and see Ellie coming up to me—Ellie and Carlton.

I give Carlton a look as I slap his hand. We hug real quick. I'm feeling good, so I even give Ellie a quick hug.

"You went *off*," Carlton says to me.

"Forty-two points, yo!" We slap hands again, both of us grinning. "Most I ever scored in one game."

"You keep going like that—"

"Yeah," I say before he can even finish. "Put Percy on the map finally. How's Tech doing?"

"We doing okay," Carlton says.

"They're doing more than okay," Ellie says. "Won their last four games."

I look from one to the other, then back again, and raise my eyebrows.

Carlton smiles. "Nah, man," he says. "It's not like that. We're friends."

Ellie looks confused for a minute, then she smiles.

"Oh," I say. "That's what they calling it these days."

People start pouring out of Percy, moving around us, slapping my hand and telling me what a good game I had.

"Yo—thanks for coming, but I gotta get out of this cold."

Ellie looks at me. "Maybe you can come and get a bite with us or something. We're going to the diner around the corner. Nothing big."

Carlton starts jumping up and down, his hands in his pockets. "You know—a little warm-up before we head across that bridge."

"Nah, man," I say. "I'm not into that third-wheel thing. You know how 'friends' be acting."

Ellie rolls her eyes. "It's not like that, Kennedy."

"True that," Carlton says, grinning. "I'm gay, man. Can you handle that?"

I look at him, then take a step back. "Hey, it ain't nothing. You know. It takes all kinds and all." Then after a minute, I say, "Damn. For real, man?"

Carlton nods. "And no offense, Kennedy, but you're not my type."

I stand there a minute, trying to let stuff sink in.

"I mean, it don't mean anything to me, but—like, for real, *gay*?"

Carlton just looks at me.

"Damn," I say again. "Whatever. That's *your* thing." Then it hits me. "Yo! Were you and Miah like . . . together—"

"Kennedy!" Ellie says. But she's smiling. "C'mon. I was the one with Miah, remember? Hello?"

I shrug. "You know. Sometimes brothers go both—"

"Don't even," Ellie says.

Carlton shakes his head. "Nah, man," he says. "Me and Miah were friends. Believe it or not, straight guys and gay guys can hang without it being a thing."

"I know that. What—you think you're the first gay boy I ever talked to or something?"

Carlton just kinda smiles. "How would I know? We're just getting to know each other."

"Well, you're not. I don't live under some rock or something. I've seen some things." I thought about all the gay brothers at my church—*I* knew they were gay whether they were calling it that or not. And my uncle James is gay—and not scared to tell anybody.

"Anyway," Ellie says. "Tonight is ..." She hugs herself and looks around a bit. "You know, the night Miah died."

I feel the wind leave me a little bit. I feel myself starting to sweat, even in the cold.

None of us says anything. People keep moving around us and I hear *Good game, Kennedy* again and again, but the words sound like they're coming from far away. I hear myself cursing again.

"You coming?" Carlton asks.

"Yeah, let's at least go get some fries or something," I say. "Show a dead brother some love."

"That dead brother probably helped you get that ball in the basket all those times," Carlton says.

"Well, I'm all for that." I give Carlton another look. I want to say, *The way you play ball, man—you sure you're gay?* But I'd had enough with that conversation for one night.

Carlton puts his arm around Ellie's shoulder.

"It's like *crazy* stars out tonight," he says.

And me and Ellie and him look up. And keep on looking.

Nelia

WINTER NOW. I TRY NOT TO MARK THE DAYS. HE GOT SHOT on a Saturday in December. We buried him that Monday. I closed the date book on my writing desk a long time ago. Over a year has passed since Miah died. The date book is black with gold letters on the front—*Remember*, it says. And I do.

It's snowing this morning. I stand at the window and watch the white flakes come down, sprinkle themselves over the block like someone's chenille bedspread. I eat a fried egg sandwich standing, look up at the silvered sky.

And remember.

The first third of my book is done now. There is a little girl telling the story—a ghost named Annabelle. Do I believe in ghosts? Now I do. Annabelle walks through this house and across my pages and tells her story. I listen and write it down—and in her story are the stories of people

I've known and people I hope to meet one day. One day someone will read this book and maybe it will make them laugh. Or cry. Who knows. All I know is what I have here—a third of a finished book, a girl named Annabelle, black print on white paper, a new world to walk into.

The writing comes to me and I let it. Some days it is so filled with sadness that I have to lie down, sleep, forget for a while. Some days there is an absolute joy to it.

Some days there is Ellie in my kitchen, the yellow-gold light spilling over us as we talk. Some evenings there is Norman on my stoop, telling me about his life, listening to me talk about mine—friends now, the past of us together not as painful as it once was. And on Saturdays there is Carlton, carrying my grocery bags—when I say, *Sing, Carlton*, he does, and his soft voice takes me back to another time, a lighter time, a freer time.

And each day there is at least one perfect moment—the way the sun moves around the living room, roasted potatoes with lots of rosemary and oil, a new baby wrapped up in blue, a child laughing.

The snow blows and blows. I turn away from my window, make my way upstairs to my study. When I turn my lamp on, so much beautiful light fills the room.

Ellie

WHAT SURPRISES ME STILL IS HOW MUCH DOESN'T CHANGE. You go outside and the night sky is still night sky—moon waxing and waning, stars—some brighter than others. Day means clouds or no clouds, rain or no rain. Cold or hot. You sweat. You cry. You walk and eat and pull your socks up when they fall down. You lace up your boots or strap on your sandals. You walk into a store and buy a new shirt. A day or two later you wear it and somebody says, *Hey, nice shirt. Is it new?*

You go days without remembering and then for days you can't forget. But your smile comes more often. And the world seems to open its arms to you.

You laugh with Carlton. You have long, deep conversations with Nelia, you begin to talk more with Kennedy—whose smile, when it comes, is like a small gift.

You sit some mornings and think about what those

who leave us leave behind—this . . . this potential for a new life . . . a different life. This *gift* of a future that we never imagined, filled with people we might have otherwise overlooked.

This morning there is so much snow on the ground. I walk slowly to Central Park. When I get to the entrance, I feel my heart start to beat hard. But I keep walking. The park is empty and still. The branches dip down with the weight of the snow.

Then I get to the place where Miah fell and wait for my screaming to come. But it doesn't. Instead the wind lifts up, blowing my hair into my eyes. Blowing the snow up around me. I listen to the sound it makes. *Shhhh. Shhhh. Shhhh.*

"Jeremiah Roselind," I whisper. "I will *always* remember you."

The wind takes my words, lifts them gently into the air.

"Always," I say again.

And the wind moves softly across my cheeks. Tender as a hand.

Jeremiah

ELLIE EISEN. I WILL ALWAYS REMEMBER YOU.

When you die, you turn away from the world you've always known and begin the long, slow walk into the next place. And behind you—everyone you left is taking a step deeper into their new world. The world they're learning to live in without you.

When you die, your voice becomes the wind and whispers to the living—

Ellie. You're loved.

Carlton. You're loved.

Mama. You're loved.

Pops. You're loved.

And Kennedy—hey, Kennedy—you got game, yo!

And when each of the people you left behind has heard,

you turn slowly and begin your long walk into *your* new world.

But some every now and then you stop, look behind you.

And remember.